WILLIE
IN THE
BIG WORLD

WILLIE IN THE BIG WORLD

An adventure with numbers

SVEN NORDQVIST

WILLIAM MORROW & COMPANY,INC.
NEW YORK

1   2   3   4   5   6   7   8   9   10

Library of Congress Cataloging-in-Publication Data
Nordqvist, Sven.   Willie in the big world.   Translation of: Minus och stora världen. Summary: In searching for the big world, Willie encounters witches, talking animals, and other strange creatures, who give him odd objects that come in handy later on, and introduce him to the concepts of numbers and counting.
[1. Fantasy.   2. Counting]   1. Title.
PZ7.N7756Wi 1986   [E]   85-15307
ISBN 0-688-06142-7
ISBN 0-688-06143-5 (lib. bdg.)

WILLIE IN THE BIG WORLD

"I'm going out into the big world to see what it's like," said Willie one day.

"All right son," said his mother, "but don't stay away too long."

Before he left, Willie went to say good-bye to Grandfather and his pig.

"You need to take something with you on your trip," said Willie's grandfather. "Here, take my right shoe. It'll bring you success in the big world. I've had it for thirty years, and I've got a house and a pig."

"Thanks very much," said Willie.

"Off with you now and good luck on your travels," said Grandfather.

So Willie went off to see the big world. He had only one thing with him: a shoe.

He hadn't been on the road very long when he met an old woman. She had two hats on her head and two pairs of shoes on her feet. When she saw Willie she stopped and stared. "You've only got one shoe," she shrieked.

"No, I've got three," said Willie. "My regular ones and this one that I got from my grandfather. It will bring me success in the big world."

"If you're going into the big world you should always have two of everything, in case you lose one. I'll have to see if I've got an extra shoe."

The old woman started to rummage through her two paper bags. She took out two thermos bottles, two towels, two alarm clocks, and a pile of other things. But she did not have an extra shoe.

"Take this instead," she said, handing Willie a spool of thread. Willie thanked her and went on his way.

Now he had two things with him in the big world: a shoe and a spool of thread.

A little while later, Willie heard branches breaking in the forest. From between the trees burst three nomads riding camels.

"Can you tell us where we can get water for our animals?"

"The gardener who lives over there has a hose," said Willie pointing.

"Oh, thank you," the nomads said. "For your help you may have a wish."

"I wish for a horse," said Willie. "A white one with black spots."

In a flash, a toy beaver appeared before him.

"There's a nice little horse," said the nomads. "Now we must continue our journey. Farewell."

Willie looked at the toy beaver. You could wind it up with a key so it jumped around and beat its tail on the ground. It wasn't quite as nice as a horse would have been, but now Willie had three things with him in the big world: a shoe, a spool of thread, and a toy beaver.

Willie was walking along the road when he ran into a four-headed babbler.

"Hello, boy! Hello, hello. Nice to meet you. Hello there, very nice!" babbled the babbler. "Would you like a banner? Nice, eh? Nice banner, nice beaver, nice shoe!" said the four heads together.

And before Willie could say a word, the babbler gave him the banner and ran off.

Now Willie had four things with him in the big world: a shoe, a spool of thread, a toy beaver, and a banner.

Farther down the road, Willie heard shouting and laughter coming from a big garden. He ran over.

"Five cheers for the flag-maker. Hip, hip, hooray!" It was the flag-maker's birthday. Four of his friends were celebrating by hoisting him up and down the flagpole.

"Now it's time for tea and cake in the garden,"
he cried as he slid down the pole with a bump.
Willie went, too.

It was a jolly party, and Willie ate as much cake
as he wanted. In the center of the cake stood five
little tin flagpoles. Willie was given one of them.

Now Willie had five things with him in the big
world: a shoe, a spool of thread, a toy beaver, a
banner, and a flag.

Willie followed the road into a dark woods. A witch was sitting on a rock, stirring something in a pot and singing:

"A viper at the bottom, two cross-eyed mice, three black magpies crawling with lice, four big pinches of powdery snuff, five bottles of ink, and that's enough." Then she let out a loud cackle and gobbled up all the soup.

"Lower your eyes and flex your nose, flap your ears and away she goes," the witch chanted. Then she turned into two big sails that swept off and disappeared over the woods.

Might be handy to have that pot, thought Willie, taking it. Now he had six things with him in the big world: a shoe, a spool of thread, a toy beaver, a banner, a flag, and a pot.

Willie walked in the meadow down by a lake. A girl sat picking flowers as she sang a song.

"I'm picking seven different kinds of flowers," she said. "I'm going to put them under my pillow so I can dream of the person who will be my dearest friend."

Willie picked a large bunch of dandelions and gave it to the girl.

"Now I must go," he said. "I'm off to see the big world."

Eight animals had gathered along the side of the road—a fox, a hedgehog, a hare, a beetle, a tiger, a snake, an elk, and an owl that was sitting on the elk's antlers. They were watching an old television without a screen. Inside the television sat a mouse in a pot.

"Welcome, everyone, to *Animal Jackpot!*" said the mouse. "Here's the first question. How many corners on a cube?"

"Are you hungry?" bawled the hedgehog, who was slightly deaf.

"No," said Willie, who was still stuffed with birthday cake. "I just ate."

"Eight! That's correct!" yelled the mouse. "A cube has eight corners. Come out and get your prize." All the animals clapped. The mouse handed the prize to Willie—a pencil sharpener in the shape of a globe. "And that's all from 'TV Eight' today," said the mouse, pulling a windowshade down over the hole.

Now Willie had eight things with him in the big world: a shoe, a spool of thread, a toy beaver, a banner, a flag, a pot, a blue forget-me-not, and a pencil sharpener shaped like a globe.

When Willie had come out of the forest and was halfway down the slope, he heard loud cackling. Nine geese flapped and honked along dragging a washtub on wheels. In the tub sat a little man dressed in elegant clothes. He pulled the tub to a halt and pointed at Willie.

"I'm a duke," the little man said. "I've got nine proud steeds and a silver coach. People bow when I approach. Come on now, bow," he commanded as he reached out with his hand. He didn't notice that he dropped his silk handkerchief.

Willie bent down to pick it up. "Good," said the count triumphantly. "There's still respect for royalty. I'm off!" He cracked his whip, and before Willie could return the handkerchief, off they went.

Now Willie had nine things with him in the big world: a shoe, a spool of thread, a toy beaver, a banner, a flag, a pot, a forget-me-not, a pencil sharpener shaped like a globe, and a silk handkerchief.

Farther down the road Willie found a big net. Just as he started to pick it up he heard a voice boom:

"That is my hairnet. I wear it when I'm asleep so my ten hairs don't get ruffled." A giant was standing before him pointing at the net with his huge finger.

"It's mine now because I found it," said Willie.

"Now listen here—" said the giant.

But Willie grabbed the hairnet and darted into the forest. The giant ploughed on after him as fast as he could, but Willie soon lost him.

Now Willie had ten things with him in the big world: a shoe, a spool of thread, a toy beaver, a banner, a flag, a pot, a forget-me-not, a pencil sharpener shaped like a globe, a silk handkerchief, and a hairnet.

After Willie had been walking for a time, he wondered whether this really was the right way to the big world. Then he saw a tiny fisherman looking sad.

"My sailboat has disappeared," said the fisherman. "I live on the island out there. How am I going to get home?"

"You can have this shoe for a boat," said Willie. "And here's a banner for a sail and a tin flag for a rudder."

"How can I thank you?" said the fisherman. "Do you want a fish?"

"No, thanks," said Willie. "Can you tell me which path leads to the big world?"

"It's the path with the yellow stones. When you've passed a hundred you're there." Willie waved good-bye and continued along the path. When Willie had counted thirty yellow stones the path split. Now he did not know which way to go.

Then he heard a little dressmaker grumbling.
"The queen has ordered me to make a ball gown
for her dog. What am I to do?"

"I've got a nice piece of silk," said Willie, taking out the
duke's handkerchief. "Here's a spool of thread, and you can
use this toy beaver as a tailor's dummy."

"Oh, that looks just like the queen's dog," she said. "How
can I thank you?"

"Just tell me which path leads to the big world," said
Willie.

"It's that one there," said the dressmaker. "When you've
counted seventy yellow stones, you're there."

When Willie had counted thirty stones he came to another fork in the road where a tiny explorer stood looking up into a big tree. "My balloon is stuck in the tree," he said sadly.

"You can have this net, and I've got a pot you can use as a basket," said Willie. They packed the balloon into the hairnet and tied it to the pot. The explorer got ready to cast off.

"Wait," cried the explorer. "I don't have a map."

Willie threw him the pencil sharpener shaped like a globe.

"Which way to the big world?" he shouted after him. But the explorer didn't hear. He was busy examining the hole in the globe where you put the pencil in.

"A black hole at the South Pole," the explorer called. "I must get there immediately!"

Willie went down the road where the yellow stones were lying three by three. When he had counted up to ninety stones, the road narrowed to a path. There were supposed to be a hundred stones. Had he gone the wrong way? The path led down to the town where he lived. He could see his house. There were only ten stones left to get to the big world. He could always go on tomorrow. Willie was getting hungry, so he went right home. He put his little blue forget-me-not in the window of his room. From his window he couldn't see the yellow stones in the road, but he knew they were there.